CHRISTOPHER'S
FIRST CHRISTMAS

STEPHANIE JEFFS
ILLUSTRATED BY JACQUI THOMAS

Everywhere Joe went,
Christopher Bear went, too.
One day Joe went to preschool.
There were twinkling lights on the playhouse.
And the hobby horse was eating hay from a bag.
"It's because it's nearly Christmas,"
Miss Rosie said.

5

6

Joe and Harry sat at the table with scissors and glue.
"Today we're making shiny stars," said Miss Rosie.
Harry and Joe worked very hard.
Christopher Bear did, too.
"Look at my star!" said Harry.
It was big and covered in glitter.
Christopher Bear just smiled
his crooked smile
made of button thread.

Joe went to play with the farm.

Elizabeth was counting the sheep.

"Look at the baby lambs!" she said.

And she gave one to Christopher Bear to hold.

"I've got a new baby brother," said Elizabeth.

"But I'm not allowed to hold him yet."

8

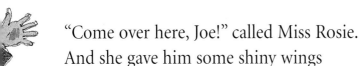

"Come over here, Joe!" called Miss Rosie.
And she gave him some shiny wings
from the dress-up box.

Joe and Christopher Bear danced together.
"We're flying!" said Joe.

11

"We're going to have our story soon,"
said Miss Rosie.
"But first of all, I need some help."
She rummaged in the dress-up box.
"You can be Mary," she said,
giving Elizabeth a blue cloak.
"And you can be Joseph," she said to Ben.
She put a tea towel on his head.

12

"Here's your donkey."

Miss Rosie gave Ben the hobby horse.

"Joe and Elizabeth can help me fill the cot with straw."

They carried the cot to the story mat.

Christopher Bear went along for the ride.

14

15

All the children sat on the story mat.
"This is the story of the very first Christmas,"
began Miss Rosie.
"Long ago, on the very first Christmas night,
a bright star twinkled in the sky."
Harry held up his star for everyone to see.

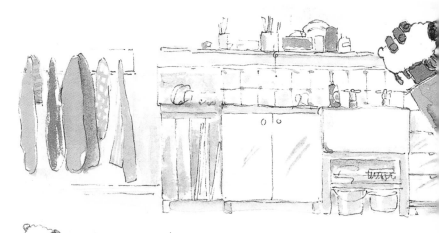

"On the first Christmas night," said Miss Rosie, "there were shepherds looking after their sheep outside a town called Bethlehem."
Jessie and Oliver held up the sheep and lambs.

18

19

"Angels sang in the sky that night,"
said Miss Rosie, "because something
very special had happened."
Joe stood up, and showed everyone his wings.
"On the very first Christmas," said Miss Rosie,
"God sent his Son to be born as a baby."

21

Miss Rosie held out her hand to Ben and Elizabeth.
"Mary and Joseph had traveled a long way,
but at last they came to Bethlehem.
Mary was going to have a baby," said Miss Rosie.
"But there was no room for them to stay at the inn."

"That night Mary had her baby in a stable, and she made him a bed in the manger."
Just then, Elizabeth's mommy came into preschool.
She was carrying Elizabeth's new baby brother.
She put the baby gently into the cot full of straw.

"Who was the baby in the manger?" whispered Joe.
"It was Jesus," replied Miss Rosie, "God's Son."

All the children looked at the baby.

Everyone was quiet, thinking about the baby Jesus, God's Son, sleeping in a manger.

Joe squeezed Christopher Bear.

And Christopher Bear just smiled his crooked smile made of button thread.

29

Large-quantity purchases or custom editions of this book are available at a discount from the publisher. For more information, contact the sales department at Augsburg Fortress, Publishers, 1-800-328-4648, or write to: Sales Director, Augsburg Fortress, Publishers, P.O. Box 1209, Minneapolis, MN 55440-1209.

First Augsburg Books edition. Originally published as *Christopher Bear's First Christmas* copyright © 2002 AD Publishing Services Ltd. 1 Churchgates, The Wilderness, Berkhamsted, Herts HP4 2UB

ISBN 0-8066-4349-8
AF 9-4349
First edition 2002

02   03   04   05   06   1   2   3   4   5   6   7   8   9   10